R. J. Barnes had never though... ... ...
a great book reader, the idea of writing a book had never been
dreamt of.

The inspiration to write this book came on a trip to Krakow
(Poland) in February 2016. Reading about the Wawel Dragon
conjures up magical and mystical stories. In the market place
there were many stalls and that's where the cheeky face of
Arrek was discovered. Thoughts of this character and the fun
he could have continued to play on the author's mind, until
pen met paper and a book was written.

The Adventures of Arrek the Dragon

R.J. Barnes

The Adventures of Arrek the Dragon

Nightingale Books

NIGHTINGALE PAPERBACK

A CIP catalogue record for this title is
available from the British Library.

ISBN 978 1 912021 62 8

*Nightingale Books is an imprint of
Pegasus Elliot MacKenzie Publishers Ltd.*
www.pegasuspublishers.com

First Published in 2017

**Nightingale Books
Sheraton House Castle Park
Cambridge England**

Printed & Bound in Great Britain

Acknowledgments

To the motley crew, who ventured with me into Poland in January 2016, Sue, Alan, Heather, Tom and Jen. For the advice given on buying a cuddly dragon, and the mischief he got up to during the time we were there. All this gave me the inspiration to write this book.

I should also mention Lillie Lovell (age 9), daughter of a client, and dear friend. Lillie has read the book a number of times in its early days, corrected my mistakes and vetted all the pictures. For Lillie's help I'm truly grateful.

Chapter 1: Arrek Arrives

Alex went into the kitchen.

"Mummy, when will Daddy be home?" she asked.

"He will be back today," Mummy said.

Daddy was an engineer and sometimes went abroad on business. This time Daddy had been away for a week in a city called Krakow in Poland.

Alex was excited because when Daddy came back from a trip, he always brought Alex a present. Last time it was a cuddly teddy bear holding a bright red heart. Alex wondered what it would be this time.

Daddy arrived home at six thirty. By now Alex was jumping up and down with excitement.

"What have you got? What have you got for me, Daddy?" Alex squealed.

"Calm down, Alex," Daddy said. "I have your present wrapped up safely in my case." Daddy went to the hall and brought in his suitcase and lifted it up onto the table. Alex couldn't see, so she climbed up on the chair and peered over the edge. Deep in the case, surrounded by soft cloths, there was a box, quite a big box. Alex was getting more excited as Daddy pulled it out and handed it to her.

"What is it?" cried Alex.

Daddy handed Alex the box, telling her to be very careful not to drop it as it might break. Alex took it, sat at the table and opened it, taking out a lot of soft paper. She saw what looked like a funny-shaped ball inside.

"What is it, Daddy?" Alex asked.

Daddy said, "It's a magic light for your bedroom." Alex now had it right out of the box. It was a strange shape, sort of oval with a flat bottom and it stood perfectly upright. The colours were amazing, being both blue and white – making a marbled effect, – and it gently glowed.

"It's beautiful!" cried Alex. "Where did you get it, Daddy?"

"I was walking in the old square in Krakow on my way to dinner," said Daddy, "when I saw a small passageway with a shop at the end. It was very dark, but I seemed to be drawn toward the light that was over the door. There were lots of unusual things in the window, so I went in for a look. A nice old man asked if he could help me, so I told him all about you, and that I wanted a special present for my Alex. The man asked me if you were kind, gentle and a very good little girl. I told him you were and he went to a drawer where he had three of these," said Daddy, pointing to the light. "He said they were magic and would, once in your bedroom, be warm and glow," Daddy said to Alex. "There is just one strange thing the man said: he made me make a promise that, if ever the light broke, you must still look after all the pieces and keep it safe always. So, as I promised the man, you must promise me."

Alex said, "I will, Daddy, I promise!" And with that she jumped down from the table and took her new present to her room.

Alex put the new light on her bedside table. It was just getting dark and it gave off a blue glow. She closed the curtains and went down for dinner – fish fingers and chips, her favourite.

After dinner, Mummy said, "Alex, it's time for you to go to bed. Go up and clean your teeth, and I will come up and tuck you in and read you a bedtime story."

Alex went up and checked her new lamp – it was brighter now, giving off a soft glow and lighting up the room. She then went to clean her teeth. Back in her room she got undressed and jumped into bed.

Ten minutes later, Mummy called, "Are you in bed, Alex?"

"Yes, Mummy!" replied Alex, and Mummy came up to read her a bedtime story. Tonight it was all about a princess and a dragon. Mummy told great stories and she was soon asleep.

Alex awoke to the sound of a strange noise. She looked at the clock. It was just after three in the morning. The noise was like a soft rumbling noise and it seemed to be coming from the new lamp. Alex leaned over and gave it a gentle tap, the noise stopped, so she turned over and went back to sleep.

Alex was up early in the morning to get ready for school, as Daddy was going to drop her off on his way to work. She ate her breakfast, got her bag, kissed Mummy goodbye and skipped off to join Daddy in the car.

On the way to work Alex said, "Daddy, I love my new light. Thank you. It gives off a lovely glow in my room, but…"

"But what?" asked Daddy.

"I woke up at three o'clock this morning because there was a strange noise in my room."

"What sort of noise?" asked Daddy.

"Well, it was a sort of rumbling noise coming from the new lamp."

"Are you sure?" Daddy asked.

"Oh yes!" said Alex. "I gave it a gentle tap and it stopped!"

"I think you were dreaming after Mummy telling you the story! I'm sure it won't happen again." And as Daddy said that, he pulled up outside school. Alex kissed him goodbye and went to join her friends in class.

Alex was excited when she entered her classroom and wanted to tell all her friends and the teacher about the amazing present Daddy had brought her from Poland, but every time she tried, something inside stopped her. She didn't know why but thought it best she kept it as a secret.

The day seemed to go so slowly and all Alex wanted to do was get home to check on her very special lamp. Three o'clock arrived at last and Alex skipped out of the school to meet Mummy who was waiting outside. Alex jumped into the car and strapped herself in. "Have you had a nice day at school?" asked Mummy.

"It was okay," replied Alex.

"Did you tell your friends about your new lamp?"

"No!" Alex replied, "I think I want to keep it a secret."

"Why is that?" Mummy asked.

"I don't know, it just seems the right thing to do," said Alex.

Mummy parked the car in the drive. Alex jumped out and ran inside and up to her room to check on the lamp. It sat there on the bedside table softly glowing with a very slight hum coming from it. As Alex touched it the humming stopped.

The next couple of weeks everything went on as normal, except the lamp was slowly changing colour. No longer was it blue and white, although it still looked like marble. It was now very pinkish and felt definitely warmer than when it had first arrived.

One night, when Alex went to bed, Mummy said to Daddy, "Darling, I'm a little worried about Alex's lamp."

"Why is that?" asked Daddy.

"Well, it's definitely changing and, if it should break, Alex will be heart-broken. I thought that perhaps when you're back in Poland next week, you should go back to the shop and get another one, so we have a spare if anything should happen to the one upstairs."

"That's not a bad idea," said Daddy. "I will go and see the man and get another one."

On Sunday, Alex and Mummy took Daddy to the airport, and off he went again to Krakow in Poland. He would be back on Friday so not long to wait for another present!

The week dragged by for Alex as it always did when Daddy was away, but every night as she looked at the light she thought of him and that he would be home soon, and every night the light looked a little redder in colour and the humming got louder.

Alex went to school on Friday excited, knowing that, at five o'clock, she and Mummy would be heading off to the airport to get Daddy.

They reached the arrivals hall at six thirty. Daddy was due through any time.

"Don't pester Daddy for a present, Alex," said Mummy. "Wait till we get home."

Daddy came through ten minutes later and Alex rushed up to him, giving him a big cuddle.

"Daddy! Daddy! I have to tell you: my lamp is really red now and very warm! It looks even more beautiful than when you bought it!"

"Hmmm!" said Daddy. "That's very strange."

"Why is that, darling?" Mummy asked.

"I will tell you later," said Daddy.

And with that they all set off for home.

This time Daddy had brought some special Polish sweets for Alex.

"You can have two tonight," Daddy said, "and then off to bed."

"Please read me a story, Daddy." So off they went upstairs together.

"Tonight's story is about a princess and a friendly dragon." said Daddy, and he started telling Alex of a Princess who had great adventures with her best friend, a dragon. Alex was soon asleep and, as Daddy got up to leave the room, he thought he heard a noise from the lamp, but he told himself that he was imagining it and went downstairs.

"Did you get another lamp, darling?" enquired Mummy.

"No," said Daddy. "It's all very strange. I went back to the shop but it wasn't there!"

"You mean it was shut?" said Mummy.

"No, it wasn't there! I asked a number of other shop owners and they said that there had never been a shop there, but it was definitely the place where I went before. I just don't understand it!" said Daddy.

As he said that, there was a loud CRACK and a bright light lit up Alex's room and the hall.

Daddy rushed out of the kitchen, calling, "Alex, are you all right?"

"Yes," murmured Alex, "but I think you had better come up, something has happened to my light!"

Alex was sat on the edge of the bed when Mummy and Daddy entered the room.

"I think he is friendly!" said Alex.

Mummy and Daddy gasped. -There on the bedside table was the lamp split in two, with a white glow all around it, and there in the middle sat a small green dragon with a bright orange chest, gently blowing small smoke rings from his nostrils.

Chapter 2: Learning to live with a dragon

Mummy and Daddy rubbed their eyes in disbelief, but the little dragon was still sitting there, blowing small smoke rings into the air. As Daddy was just about to speak, the dragon walked to the edge of the bedside table and hopped on to Alex's lap. Alex sat bolt upright, but the dragon rubbed his head against her, snuggled up on her lap and went to sleep.

Alex whispered, "He seems to like me!"

"You were the first person that he saw when he hatched; he probably thinks that you are his mummy," Daddy explained.

"What are we going to do?" asked Mummy.

"He's a dragon! I want to keep him!" said Alex.

With that the shell started to glow white. Inside, it was sort of slowly going from a soft light to a bright light. Daddy picked up one half of the shell.

"It has writing in it!" said Daddy.

"What does it say?" whispered Mummy and Alex together.

Daddy started to read what was written inside the shell. "*Alex, you have been specially chosen.*"

"How does it know my name?" interrupted Alex.

"I can't answer that." said Daddy and continued to read the message. "*Alex, you have been specially chosen to be the keeper of this baby dragon currently asleep on your knee. His name is Arrek, great grandson of Ninarth the Dragon Lord and son of Kelarth the Great from Poland.*

"*Arrek has been in his shell for many years, waiting for the right person to be his keeper. Alex, your daddy said that you were kind, gentle and a very good little girl, just what Arrek needs. He will be very loyal and will always be your friend, but you will need to teach him everything – don't forget that he is only a baby dragon.*

"This must be a magic shell too," said Daddy. "As I'm reading the message, it's scrolling down with more information!"

More writing appeared in the shell. Daddy continued reading the message to Alex and Mummy: "*Yes, I am a magic shell. My name is Noroth, Guardian of all Dragons. You must keep both pieces of the shell forever, for if you should lose or destroy either part of the shell, I won't be able to communicate with you and Arrek will perish.*"

"What does perish mean, Daddy?" asked Alex.

"He would die," replied Daddy, before he continued to read: "*You can ask me any questions at any time if you need help and I will give you the answers. I'm here to help the Dragon Keeper and protect Arrek.*"

"Umm… What does he eat?" asked Alex.

And, sure enough, the printing in the shell changed.

"*Arrek likes most things, a bit like a dog. He likes meat as his main diet and he will probably catch flies for fun.*" The writing changed again. "*Just one thing to remember when living with a dragon: if he should get agitated, feel threatened or scared, you will see flames shoot from his nostrils. It's a defence mechanism, nothing to be scared of, but he is a baby and will struggle to control it at first. So keep a small fire extinguisher handy and, if he gets hiccups, don't put him near anything flammable.*"

With that, the shell went dim and the writing disappeared.

Alex carefully lifted Arrek up and got into bed, putting the now gently snoring dragon close to her on the duvet.

Mummy said, "I'm not sure it's a good idea having him on the bed."

However, Daddy said, "I think it will be fine, but we will have to shut your door, Alex. Will you be okay with that?" But before Alex could answer, Daddy said "I have an idea!" and he disappeared downstairs. A few minutes later he re-appeared, fire extinguisher from the kitchen in one hand and the old baby alarm from the workshop in the other. "I fitted new batteries," said Daddy, "and it's working like new!"

Alex and Arrek were now both asleep as Mummy and Daddy closed the door and went downstairs with the baby alarm. When it was switched on, all that could be heard was Alex and Arrek both gently snoring together.

When Alex awoke the next morning, she was alone in the bed. She slowly looked around and saw Arrek sitting on the bedside table on the other side of the bed. He didn't see Alex watching him – he was concentrating really hard on a spider that was walking up the wall about thirty centimetres from his nose. All of a sudden his tongue shot from his mouth with such force, he missed the spider and toppled backwards, falling off the bedside table onto the bed. The surprise was too much for Arrek and Alex saw two small flames shoot from his nostrils.

Alex chuckled as Arrek was trying to get himself upright on the bed, but he saw the spider move and like a flash he was back on the bedside table, his tongue shot out catching the spider and both the tongue and the spider disappeared back in his mouth.

Alex clapped with excitement and Arrek looked at her as he swallowed the spider. She was sure she saw Arrek wink at her! Breakfast over, Arrek curled up on the bed and went back to sleep.

Alex put water down for Arrek and some kitchen towel in a small box as a toilet, but Arrek just stood in the water, and only used the toilet once in over a week! He just slept and occasionally caught a spider for his dinner.

After nearly two weeks of this, Alex said, "Mummy, I'm worried about Arrek. Can I ask the shell what to do?"

"That's a good idea!" said Mummy and they went off together to get it.

Daddy had found a perfect wooden box to keep the shell in and Mummy got it out of the drawer in Alex's room.

"Let me ask!" begged Alex. "Please, Mummy!"

"You can ask, dear." replied Mummy, passing the shell to her.

"Err, excuse me, Mr Shell," whispered Alex.

The shell started to glow inside and writing started to appear. 'Hello, Alex,' appeared in the shell. 'You must call me Noroth, for you and I will have to work together to ensure Arrek is always safe and happy.'

"Oh, I will, Noroth!" said Alex.

The writing in the shell changed. 'Now, how can I help you?'

"I'm worried," said Alex. "Arrek just sleeps and has the occasional meal, and won't drink. He just stands in his water."

The writing changed. 'Ahh! I should have told you about standing in water. Dragons can't swallow water, as it would put their flame out, so they soak it up through special pads in their feet! With regard to sleeping all the time, you must remember he is a baby dragon, and that's what babies do. It has been nearly two weeks; you will see him start to change very soon. So don't worry, all is fine.' And with that the writing disappeared and the glow from the shell faded away.

On Saturday what Noroth said was proven to be right. Alex was woken by crashing in her room. Arrek was jumping all around the room, knocking items off the bedside tables and dressing table.

"Arrek, what's the matter!" shouted Alex.

Arrek stopped dead in his tracks, turned and looked at Alex, then back to the wall where a fly was gliding past him. His tongue was out, missing the fly again and again and yet again! Tissues and toys were flying everywhere as Arrek chased the fly.

"Arrek, stop!" said Alex, and he did just that – he stopped and looked at Alex. She picked him up gently and showed him the fly, which, as they watched, settled on the wall. Putting Arrek down on the dressing table, his tongue flashed out and the fly was no more! Then another flew past Arrek's nose, but no panic this time – Arrek waited for it to settle and slowly approached it. When he knew he was close enough, his tongue hit it and the fly was in Arrek's mouth and gone. Arrek looked at Alex, and yes, she was sure she saw that cheeky little wink, or was she imagining it?

Arrek jumped onto Alex's lap, rubbed his head on her hand and jumped onto the floor and out the door.

"Where are you going?" called Alex, running after him.

This was the first time Arrek had taken any interest in leaving the bedroom. When Alex got onto the landing, she saw Arrek approaching the top of the stairs.

"No, Arrek!" she shouted, as Arrek skidded on the polished wooden floor just stopping short of the edge, as he wobbled on the top step, flames shot from his nostrils.

Was he going to fall down the stairs?

Chapter 3; Arrek goes exploring

Alex got to the top step and scooped Arrek up in her arms. "Oh, Arrek, you silly dragon, you must slow down!"

"Is everything all right?" shouted Mummy from downstairs.

"Yes, it was Arrek – he decided to run out of the bedroom and nearly fell down the stairs!"

"Have you got him now, dear?" asked Mummy.

"Yes, I'm giving him a cuddle, he's fine now."

Just as Alex said that, a fly buzzed past; Arrek jumped out of Alex's arms and shot down the landing into Mummy's room.

"Mummy! Mummy! You'd better come quick. Arrek has shot off after a fly into your room."

Mummy rushed up the stairs to join Alex and when she got to the door of the bedroom, what they saw made them both giggle.

"Look, Mummy, the fly is on the ceiling and Arrek is trying to use your bed as a trampoline to get to it!"

Sure enough, Arrek was bouncing up and down on the bed with his tongue shooting out, trying to get the fly. Each time he missed by about a centimetre. Exhausted, or so they thought, Arrek stopped for a rest. As he caught his breath, the fly decided to have another go.

"Mummy, the fly is trying to land on Arrek!"

Arrek snapped at the fly and chased it again, right over Mummy's dressing table. There was hairspray, lipsticks, face powder and lots of tubs of cream flying everywhere. As Arrek got to the end of the dressing table, he couldn't stop and he fell off the end, head first into the washing basket, and the fly flew out of the room.

"Are you all right, Arrek?" called Alex.

"Never mind Arrek," said Mummy, "just look at the state of my bedroom!"

With that, Arrek's head appeared out of the top of the washing basket with a pair of socks caught on his ear.

"Mummy is very cross, Arrek, you have been a very naughty dragon!" said Alex, and Arrek sunk back into the wash basket. "I think you had better stay there while I clear up the mess."

"Yes, I will get you the polish, a duster and the vacuum cleaner too."

For the next hour while Alex cleared up the mess that Arrek had made, all that could be heard from Arrek was gentle snoring coming from the washing basket.

Alex left Arrek snoring and went to clear up her room. After about an hour, Mummy, who was downstairs, heard the vacuum cleaner stop. She went to the bottom of the stairs and called up to Alex. "Have you finished, darling?"

"Yes, I think I have, Mummy; would you come and look, please?"

Mummy went upstairs and joined Alex in her room. "Well done, it looks great. Let's go and check my room and your sleepy dragon," said Mummy.

As they went in they saw two small smoke rings appear from the washing basket. Both Mummy and Alex giggled.

"You have done a very good job in both rooms, so I think a treat is called for!"

"Oh, what's the treat?" asked Alex.

"You will have to wait and see; we need to go to the shops," said Mummy. "Let's put Arrek back in your room then we can go out."

Alex popped into the bathroom to wash her hands, and came back to pick Arrek up.

Mummy asked her, "What made you go and wash your hands, Alex?"

"Well, I had your make-up and furniture polish on my hands, and I didn't want to get it on Arrek in case it made him poorly."

"Well done," said Mummy. "You did the right thing, and you're really becoming a very caring dragon keeper."

Alex gently lifted Arrek out of the washing basket and took him back to her room, putting him in his bed. As she did so, he rolled onto his back, let out a big snore and blew smoke rings into the air. She shut the bedroom door.

Alex got her coat and went out of the front door. Mummy locked the door and got into the car.

As they headed off to the shops Alex said, "Mummy, I'm a bit worried."

"Why is that?" asked Mummy.

"Well, Arrek wanted that fly for his dinner and he got so excited he missed it, so he used all his energy up and didn't get anything to eat."

"Don't worry," said Mummy, "we will get some stewing steak for the freezer and see if Arrek likes it. If we get it from the butchers, we can ask the butcher to cut it up into small pieces."

"That's great, Mummy, thank you!"

"And as a special treat, we can have your favourite – sausages, mashed potato and carrots."

"Fantastic!" said Alex. "I'm really looking forward to my dinner!"

Shopping all done, Mummy and Alex soon arrived home.

"If you bring everything in, I will put it away," said Alex.

Within half an hour, all the shopping was away and Mummy had started making dinner.

"I'm going up stairs to check on Arrek and get the shell out; I want to talk to Noroth," said Alex.

"Okay, darling," said Mummy. "Dinner will be about thirty minutes."

"Okay, thank you," said Alex and disappeared upstairs.

Arrek was still asleep when Alex got the wooden box out of the drawer and removed the shell.

"Are you there, Noroth?" asked Alex.

With that, the shell started to glow. Writing started to appear in the shell. 'Hello, Alex, is everything all right?'

"Yes everything is fine... well, sort of," replied Alex.

The writing changed. 'What is worrying you, Alex?'

"Well, Arrek decided to leave the bedroom. After making a real mess in mine, he went and wrecked Mummy's room. Why is he being so naughty?"

The shell glowed and Alex read, 'He is not being naughty, he is just learning. What I haven't told you is that Arrek can understand everything you say. You stopped him falling on the landing today.'

"How do you know that?" said Alex

'I see everything, Alex, you have to remember that he is learning every day. If he does something wrong you must explain to him what he has done and why he shouldn't do it. Do you understand, Alex?'

"Yes," said Alex. "I will try my hardest to help him learn."

'I know you will, Alex,' wrote the shell, 'and he will love the stewing steak.' And with that the shell went dark. Alex put it back in its box.

"Dinner is ready!" Mummy called up the stairs.

"Coming, Mummy!" Alex replied and, closing the door, she skipped along the landing and down the stairs.

Chapter 4: Arrek discovers lemonade

"Thank you, Mummy, for my sausages, mash and carrots. It will always be my favourite," said Alex. "I'm going up now to take Arrek his stewing steak and see if he likes it."

"All right," said Mummy, "but take it up in a small bowl, please."

"Okay, Mummy, will do," replied Alex.

With that, Alex disappeared into the kitchen and put the meat in a small bowl as instructed. The next thing Mummy heard was Alex going upstairs.

As Alex entered the room, she saw Arrek on the bedside table looking out of the window. Arrek turned and looked at Alex, his eyes brightened and he jumped on the bed to greet her. After Alex had put down the bowl, Arrek jumped into her arms, cuddling up close and giving her a big lick.

"That's the first kiss I have had, Arrek!" Alex said.

Arrek snuggled in closer and gave her another lick.

"Come on, Arrek," said Alex. "I have a surprise for you!"

Putting him down on the bed, Alex got a piece of meat from the bowl, and showed it to him. Arrek sniffed it and nudged it with his nose – it didn't move. Arrek's normal dinner normally flew past him or ran up the walls; this did smell nice, but it didn't move.

"It's your special dinner," said Alex.

Arrek put his head to one side and listened. Alex pretended to eat it, Arrek glared and with that his tongue shot from his mouth and the meat was gone. Alex jumped but to her surprise she hadn't felt his tongue on her fingers, and didn't even realise that the meat had gone until she saw Arrek chewing it.

'Well he seems to like it,' thought Alex as Arrek swallowed the first piece. He spotted a second piece in the bowl, and before Alex could say anything the tongue was out and the meat gone. Arrek jumped down off the bed and stood in his water, getting a drink. He looked over his shoulder and winked.

'Yes!' thought Alex. 'That definitely was a wink!'

Arrek got out of the water and Alex dried him off. Lifting him up, she put him in his bed, but Arrek had other ideas and jumped straight out into Alex's arms and gave her another big lick, then back to his bed and curled up for the night.

Alex got into her pyjamas, climbed into bed and whispered, "Good night, Arrek."

He turned his head, winked again and settled down to sleep.

Alex read her favourite book for a while; it was the one Daddy read bedtime stories from about the Princess and the Dragon. Alex lay there reading but soon drifted off to sleep.

Mummy came up a little later to see if all was okay. She crept in, removed the still open book off the bed, put out the light and left them both gently snoring and having nice dreams.

Alex was woken by the sound of Mummy downstairs using the vacuum cleaner. Arrek was still asleep when Alex slipped out of bed and onto the landing.

"I'm up now, Mummy!" called Alex.

"Okay, darling, is there anything you would like?"

"Mmm… can I have a glass of lemonade, please?" asked Alex.

"Yes, of course, I will bring you one up," replied Mummy.

A few minutes later Mummy came into the room; there she saw Alex cuddling Arrek and the little dragon purring like a small cat. Mummy put the lemonade on the bedside table.

"Thank you, Mummy," said Alex as Arrek approached the glass of very fizzy lemonade. "Let's watch Arrek and see what he does," said Alex.

Mummy sat on the bed. Arrek could hear the small bubbles bursting on the glass as he approached. He put his nose over the edge of the glass, only to jump back as a bubble burst on it. Arrek got closer this time, putting his head into the glass, knocking it. As he did so the lemonade erupted in a mass of bubbles hitting Arrek's nose. As he hurriedly removed his head from the glass, two small jets of flames came out of his nostrils and he shot across the bed, onto the floor and under the bedside table. All that could be seen of Arrek was the end of his tail and the occasional smoke rings.

Mummy and Alex sat on the bed laughing, waiting for Arrek to reappear. When he did, all that could be seen at first was his head over the edge of the bed.

"It's okay, Arrek," said Alex, "it's only a drink – look!" And with that Alex took a large mouthful and swallowed it. "Yum!" said Alex. "It's great, you should try some. Come on, Arrek," she said as she poured some into his clean bowl.

Arrek looked as Alex stirred it with her fingers. Then he climbed into the bowl and started to drink. Then something very strange started to happen: about every ten seconds, small flames shot from Arrek's nostrils and he started making a strange noise.

"I think you had better get him out, quick!" said Mummy. "Lay him on the bed, but mind the flames!"

Alex did as asked and put Arrek on the bed. He was rolling from side to side, making a funny sound and waving his feet about in the air. The flames went out and there was a plume of smoke which came from his nose and a sound like a sigh. He lay still, looked at Alex and winked.

"Are you all right?" asked Alex, as Arrek was still on his back, and he kicked his little feet in the air.

Alex gently touched his feet and the noise started again. When she stopped, the noise stopped. She touched them again, and again the noise started.

"What is it?" said Mummy. "What's the matter with Arrek?"

"Nothing, Mummy. I think I have a very ticklish dragon, who has also just had the hiccups!" With that, Arrek looked at them both, winked and giggled again.

Chapter 5: Arrek finds the bathroom

"Come on, you two, stop playing around," said Mummy. "It's time you cleaned your teeth and had a shower, Alex, but please remember to shut Arrek in your room."

"Yes, Mummy, I will," replied Alex and, with that, Mummy left them and went downstairs.

Alex said to Arrek, "I have to go to the bathroom now and you must be good while I'm gone."

With that, Arrek turned as a fly flew past and caught his breakfast!

Alex clapped her hands. "Well done, Arrek, you caught that one when it was flying! You are a clever little dragon."

Arrek winked and came for a quick cuddle.

Alex said, "No time for that now, I have to go. Be good, Arrek." And with that Alex headed for the bathroom.

Arrek was left alone in the room, but he really didn't want to be on his own so he jumped down onto the floor. Then something happened. Mummy was downstairs, but had opened the backdoor; as she did, there was a draught that came through the house and up the stairs.

When Alex had shut the door, it hadn't completely closed and the draught moved it slightly so that there was a very small gap. It was far too small for a baby dragon to get through, but a smart dragon could try it!

Arrek went to the door and sniffed at the gap. He then tried to get his nose in it but the gap was too small. He tried with his little paws but the door was too heavy. So Arrek looked around for something smaller and stronger. As he looked over his shoulder, he found it, just what he needed to open the door: his tail... well, the end of it, anyway.

Turning around, Arrek put his tail in the gap, it fitted! And as it was tapered and strong, he just kept moving backward, forcing his tail in, and, sure enough, the door started to move. By the time Arrek was nearly out of breath, the door was open with a gap he could get his head in. Arrek turned around and put his head in the gap. One push from his thick neck and the door opened and he was out!

In front of him was the staircase that he had nearly fallen down before. Arrek approached it with caution. The stairs had big gaps in them, only bits of wood to stand on and you could see the floor a long way below. Arrek was scared and, as he got nearer, flames shot from his nostrils. Just then he heard Alex; she was in the bathroom and the door was open. Arrek plucked up all his little dragon courage and got past the stairs; little beads of dragon sweat had now formed on his brow as he reached the door and peered in.

Alex had got her toothbrush and was squeezing toothpaste onto it and then cleaning her teeth. Arrek watched in amazement as Alex put it in her mouth and brushed her teeth hard up and down.

When she had finished cleaning her teeth, she turned and went into the shower. There was music playing in the bathroom and, with the noise from the shower, Alex didn't hear Arrek come in. He looked up at where Alex had cleaned her teeth; it was high, but a jump up on to the bath, then the unit by the hand basin, should get him there.

Arrek jumped first onto the unit where the toothpaste lay with the toothbrush. He jumped, landing on the still-open toothpaste tube, and toothpaste shot out into the hand basin. Arrek leapt up, landing on the soap and sliding into the hand basin along with the toothbrush – he now found himself with everything he needed to copy Alex.

He picked up the toothbrush. It was a good job Alex only had a small brush. He rubbed it in the toothpaste. Arrek thought that he should put lots on, as he hadn't cleaned his teeth before. He then put the brush in his mouth and started scrubbing, but something very strange started to happen. The heat from Arrek's flame chamber along with the moisture in his mouth was causing the toothpaste to foam up. Soon Arrek had foam all over his nose and around his mouth.

Alex looked out of the shower and saw the head and neck of her dragon looking over the rim of the hand basin, covered in foam and blowing bubbles instead of smoke rings. Alex jumped out of the shower and grabbed a towel.

"What are you doing, Arrek!" she cried.

With that, the startled Arrek jumped out of the hand basin, skidded along the unit and down onto the bath edge. Sliding along and wobbling from side to side, he finally fell off into the shower.

Arrek thought this was great as he was running around in the warm water and all the foam was slowly disappearing out of his nose and mouth. He watched as a big lump of foam fell off his nose and the water took it down a funny hole under his feet. Alex reached in and picked up the little dragon in a towel.

With that, Mummy walked in.

"What have you two been up to?" she asked.

"Well, Arrek must have seen me cleaning my teeth and, while I was in the shower, he decided to clean his. He was covered in foam, Mummy; he looked so funny. Then he took a shower."

"Well, you had better get him really dry," said Mummy, handing Alex her special bathrobe. Alex put it on and pulled the hood up over her wet hair and started to dry a very soggy little dragon.

"Mummy?" said Alex. "Can you do Arrek a favour?"

"What is that?" asked Mummy.

"Well, could you make a bathrobe for him like the one you made for me? It will need both arm and wing holes so he can get his wings out."

"I don't see why not," said Mummy. "We will measure him up later. I think he has tired himself out." Alex was still drying him but with the gentle rubbing of his scales, he had drifted off to sleep. Alex took him back to her room, put him to bed and got dressed.

"I'm off to breakfast now, Arrek," she whispered as she gently closed the door, but this time Alex made sure it was closed tightly shut.

Chapter 6: Arrek goes downstairs

"What would you like for breakfast?" Mummy asked.

"Just some toast, please," Alex replied.

"What have you brought the egg shell down for, Alex? Is there something wrong?"

"No," said Alex. "I just thought I would have a word with Noroth while you are making breakfast."

"Okay," said Mummy. "I will just finish dusting in here, then I will do your toast. It will be about fifteen minutes, so you can chat. I think you should go in the lounge; it's quiet there."

"Okay, Mummy, I won't be long," said Alex as she disappeared out of the room.

Alex sat on the leather sofa and opened the box. Taking the egg gently out she put it on the fleece next to her.

"Noroth, Noroth, are you there?"

The egg, as before, started to glow until the light filled the room.

'Hello, Alex,' appeared on the inside of the shell. 'How are you today?'

"I'm great," replied Alex. "Are you okay?"

'Oh, I'm very well, thank you, and I'm very happy,' was printed on the inside of the egg.

"Why is that?" asked Alex.

The writing in the shell changed. 'Because we made the right decision making you the dragon keeper. I don't think Arrek could be happier and I see you're getting kisses.'

Alex blushed and said, "Well, we are having fun together and he's learning lots."

'Yes,' said the shell. 'He is very content with you and he feels safe. That's very important for a young dragon; he must feel safe. Now, what can I help you with?' said the writing in the shell.

"Well, when we first sort of spoke, you told us about Arrek's great grandfather, Ninarth the Dragon Lord, and his father, Kelarth the Great, from Poland, but you didn't mention his grandfather. I just wondered why."

'Well, he wasn't a very nice dragon,' glowed the shell. 'People think that dragons eat people and are vicious, and one of the reasons people think this is because of Arrek's grandfather.'

"What was his name?" asked Alex.

'Erfolg the Dark,' appeared in the shell. 'He came from a great and good family. Ninarth was a great and well-respected dragon, but Erfolg's egg was given to a very bad Dragon Keeper. He was a bully and as Erfolg grew up he became a bully too. He did start a family, but then one day killed Arrek's grandmother in a fit of rage. He then moved through the countryside, terrorising everything and everybody that he came into contact with, killing many people and animals. He finally made his home in a cave at the bottom of the Wawel Hill on the outskirts of Krakow.'

"What happened to him?" asked Alex.

The shell glowed, 'The king wanted him killed but he was fierce and very big; he kept burning anyone who came near with his massive flames. One day a shoemaker's son filled a dead sheep with explosives, and Erfolg ate it and it killed him. I only tell you this, Alex, so you understand the responsibility you took on becoming a dragon keeper. It's so important that no one is frightened by Arrek. You must make him a good and great dragon like his father and great grandfather.'

"I promise that I will do my best," said Alex and, with that, the glow from the shell faded away.

"Toast is ready!" called Mummy as Alex was putting the shell away.

"Coming, Mummy!" Alex called as she headed for the kitchen.

"How was Noroth?" asked Mummy.

"He's fine. I learnt a lot today."

"Did you, dear?" said Mummy. "What did you learn?"

"I will tell you later. Can I ask a favour, please?"

"Of course you can. What is it?" asked Mummy.

"Well, I think it's time Arrek came downstairs. Do you think that will be all right?" asked Alex.

"Well, we will have to watch him and try to make sure that he doesn't get into any mischief!"

"We can do it together!" said Alex as she tucked into her toast and marmite.

After breakfast Alex went upstairs and opened the bedroom door. Arrek looked over his shoulder from his bed at Alex. He then shot out of bed and into her arms.

"Wow!" Alex said. "That was a big leap!"

The little dragon licked her and snuggled in for a cuddle.

"Arrek, I have a surprise for you!" said Alex.

The dragon looked at her and laid his head to one side, as if to listen to her every word.

"Mummy has said that you're big enough to come downstairs now and join us." And with that, she put Arrek on the floor and walked out of the bedroom, this time leaving the door open. "Come on, Arrek!" Alex called, but he was unsure.

Normally he was sneaking out and getting up to mischief, but this time he was being allowed to leave the room with Alex. He approached the door and peeped around the doorframe.

"It's okay, you're allowed to come out," said Alex.

The little dragon looked over his shoulder and walked out onto the landing. He took a few more steps towards Alex, as she stepped down on to the top step. Arrek froze and started to shake.

Alex said, "What's the matter, Arrek?" as he was now shaking even more.

Alex reached out and Arrek moved back towards the wall; he went as far back as his tail would allow him. He stopped and little drops of water came from his eyes. He gulped and let out two very weak flames.

"Arrek, you're crying!" said Alex. "You're frightened of the stairs, aren't you?"

With that, Alex walked across the landing and picked up the trembling little dragon and gave him a big cuddle. Arrek buried his face in Alex's cardigan as she slowly walked downstairs.

"Is everything all right?" asked Mummy.

"It's Arrek," said Alex. "He was really frightened of the stairs. He was shaking and started to cry, so I had to carry him."

And with that, Alex sat on the sofa with Arrek on her knee. Arrek started to look around the room. He jumped down on to the floor to explore.

There was a window just like the one upstairs and another he couldn't really see out of – it had what looked like a strange mouth below it. Just then the mouth opened and spat lots of square things at him. Arrek was startled and shot flames at the nasty thing and leapt back in to Alex's arms, shaking.

"It's only the postman!" said Mummy laughing, as she patted him on the head. She got up to get the post. "There's nothing to be afraid of, Arrek."

Arrek watched Mummy pick up the post and jumped back onto the floor. As she got the post, she knocked a bag by the side of the sofa. It was her knitting. A large ball of red wool rolled slowly across the floor, stopping a few centimetres away from Arrek.

'It's staring at me,' thought Arrek as he approached it. He touched his nose on it and it moved. He did it again and it once more moved away. Arrek tried to stop it moving by jumping on it. He wobbled as the ball of wool moved first to the left, then the right, then forwards and backwards.

Arrek's little legs were trying to keep up, moving so fast they became a blur, and eventually he fell off! Both Alex and Mummy were in fits of giggles as Arrek got to his feet, wobbling from side to side as he had made himself dizzy.

Just then everything stopped. There was a large roar and another even louder than the first. Arrek waited for the flames, as a roar like that could only be from a big dragon.

There was strange ringing in Arrek's ears as he shook his head and the room went dark as Mummy got up and went to the strange window that you couldn't see out of.

Arrek once again jumped onto Alex's lap, as Mummy opened the door. As the light shone in, there stood a large black monster with a strange shining face.

Chapter 7: Arrek meets the monster

The monster stood at the door with the sun shining down from behind it, then it spoke.

"Maureen, help me off with my helmet." (Maureen was Alex's mummy's name.)

"Oh, Dennis, you frightened poor Arrek."

"Hello, Uncle," said Alex.

"Hi, babe," said Uncle Dennis, now with the helmet gone. (Uncle Dennis spoke sort of strange like that – he said it was trendy!) "I was coming past on my motorbike and thought I would pop in and see this famous dragon. Where is the little chap?"

They looked around and found Arrek hiding behind the sofa, just the end of his tail showing and the occasional smoke ring.

"Come out!" said Alex "It's only Uncle Dennis, he has come to see you."

Arrek backed out from under the sofa and turned to look at the monster. 'Ugh!' thought Arrek, pulling himself up to his full height. 'Not so scary now, are you?' The helmet, leather gloves and jacket had gone, and there was a little man with glasses rather like Alex's daddy.

"Arrek, this is my uncle Dennis, my daddy's brother. Uncle Dennis, this is Arrek."

"Well, you're a little cutie!" said Uncle Dennis, rubbing Arrek under his chin.

"This is his first time downstairs, Uncle Dennis," said Alex.

"Is he good?" asked Uncle Dennis.

"Well, he does get into a bit of mischief," said Mummy. "But he does make us laugh and he is a very nice dragon."

Arrek blushed.

"I think he knows everything you say," said Uncle Dennis.

"I'm sure he does," said Mummy. "Would you like a drink, Dennis?"

"Love a coffee, babe," said Dennis, "and a couple of pieces of toast would go down a treat!"

"I have some nice meat pâté, if you would like some?" replied Mummy.

"That would be great," said Dennis.

"Could I have a slice too?" asked Alex.

"Three slices of toast and pâté coming up," said Mummy and off she went to the kitchen, followed by Uncle Dennis.

"There!" said Alex. "I told you there was nothing to be frightened of!"

Arrek, however, was trying to get on the ball of wool again and kept falling off. Every time he fell and landed on his back, Alex tickled him and Arrek would get the dragon giggles.

Arrek was getting bored and went to see where Mummy had gone. Alex followed through the dining room to the kitchen where Mummy and Uncle Dennis were talking. They didn't notice Arrek watching as Mummy cut the bread.

"There," said Mummy to Dennis. "Listening to you, I've cut four slices instead of three!"

"Well, you have one," said Dennis.

"No, I'm on a diet," said Mummy. "I will leave it just in case you want more."

Arrek watched as Mummy opened a door and did something; there was a soft boom as flames lit up the top inside the door. She put the bread on a metal tray and put it under the flames.

"What are you doing there, Arrek?" asked Mummy.

"He was watching you make toast," said Alex as she picked him up. Arrek gave her a big lick and they went back to the lounge.

A few minutes later, Mummy and Uncle Dennis came in with a tray of toast and pâté, with coffee for Uncle Dennis, tea for Mummy, lemonade for Alex and a bowl of fresh water for Arrek. As Mummy put Arrek's bowl down, he jumped in, making quite a splash, and everybody giggled.

"Thank you, Arrek!" said Mummy, whose hand was now very wet.

Alex explained to Uncle Dennis that Arrek drank through his feet.

"Is that right, babe?" said Uncle Dennis, being what he thought was cool.

They all sat down to eat their pâté on toast and Alex offered Arrek a small piece. He sniffed the meat pate.

'It smells nice,' thought Arrek and the tongue had it out of Alex's fingers; before she could say anything else to him, it was gone and he winked at her.

"I'm sure I just saw that dragon wink," said Uncle Dennis.

"Did you, Uncle?" But Alex didn't let on that she knew!

Then Arrek jumped out of the bowl.

"Watch, Uncle!" said Alex as Arrek moved across the carpet.

"What's he doing?" asked Uncle Dennis.

"See the spider on the fireplace?" said Alex. "Just watch it."

Arrek moved closer, the tongue flashed out and the spider was gone.

"Bravo!" said Uncle Dennis. "He sure is a fast little fella."

As Arrek had his spider, they all ate their toast and drank their drinks.

While Alex was eating, Arrek went around the side of the sofa. Alex was watching him as he came face to face with the monster's head – namely, Uncle Dennis's helmet and his boots. Arrek jumped up sitting on top on the boots with his feet dangling in them. Alex was giggling. He winked at her; he was pretending that he was wearing them. As he jumped out he knocked the helmet and fell in to it as it rolled over. It came to rest on the carpet the right way up with Arrek looking out through the visor. Everybody roared with laughter and Uncle Dennis said it was the funniest thing he had ever seen in a crash helmet!

Uncle Dennis finished his coffee and said it was time to fly. Arrek thought this strange, as he hadn't got any wings.

"It must be Uncle Dennis being cool," Arrek said to himself.

Mummy and Alex were busy helping him get into his gear and talking to him as Arrek slipped from the room.

Through the dining room and into the kitchen he trotted. He did like the pâté, he thought, as he looked up at the kitchen worktop.

'Mmm, yes, I think I can get up there,' and, with that, he jumped onto the waste bin and then onto the worktop. 'What did Mummy do?' he thought. 'Cut the bread... well, that's done... then put flames on it... now, that's easy for a dragon.'

Arrek stood back, aimed at the bread and breathed out hard. Sure enough, flames shot from his nostrils and hit the bread. In a second, it was black and there was a loud beeping sound above his head.

He heard people running and shouting. Arrek panicked and shot backwards, landing in the bread bin and the front rolled down shut. When Mummy, Uncle Dennis and Alex entered the kitchen, it was full of smoke. Uncle Dennis opened the window and Mummy stopped the smoke alarm. As the kitchen cleared, all that could be seen was a very blackened, burnt piece of toast but no Arrek.

Panic set in and Alex called, "Arrek, where are you?"

They couldn't see him anywhere. Then it happened – the bread bin started to jump about. Uncle Dennis opened it and there was a small dragon with a very black, sooty face.

Uncle Dennis said, "I see what you mean about mischief!"

They all laughed. Alex picked up Arrek.

Uncle Dennis said that he had to fly. He kissed every one and left, saying, "Stay cool, folks!"

'Weird!' thought Alex.

There was a loud roar and he was gone.

'Must have been riding a dragon!' Arrek thought. 'Pity I didn't meet it.'

Mummy said, "You'd better take him upstairs and clean him up, while I sort the kitchen out."

"Yes, Mummy," said Alex and disappeared up the stairs with Arrek, making sure to cover his eyes.

Chapter 8: Arrek gets his new robe

Mummy called up the stairs to Alex, "Before you put Arrek in the shower, I want to measure him for his robe."

"Okay, Mummy. Are you coming up now?"

"Yes, I'm just getting my tape measure," she replied.

Mummy appeared at the bathroom door and, as she looked in, she saw Alex teaching Arrek how to brush his teeth properly.

"Hi, Mummy," said Alex. "I'm just showing Arrek how to brush his teeth."

"I guessed that," said Mummy.

Arrek was brushing his big fangs up and down.

"Rinse your mouth now," said Alex, and Arrek put his mouth under the tap, filled it with water and spat it into the sink.

"Well done, Arrek," said Mummy. "Now stand still and let me measure you." Mummy gave Alex a note pad and pencil. "Can you write the measurements down, please?"

"Yes, Mummy," said Alex.

Mummy got her tape measure and Arrek stood up straight while Mummy called out the measurements to her.

"Right, I'm off to get the sewing machine out and make his robe while you clean him up."

"That's great, Mummy," said Alex. "Thank you."

With that, Mummy disappeared downstairs.

"Okay, Arrek, it's time for your shower."

Arrek was jumping up and down with excitement. The shower was large and round and was about ten centimetres deep to stop the water coming out. Alex lifted Arrek into the shower and turned the water on. Arrek was running around like a mad thing under the warm water and then he saw it – an oval bar of soap which was moving in the flow of the water. Arrek charged at it and jumped, landing right in the middle. The speed at which he launched himself at the soap and the force of the water's flow sent it flying forwards at speed.

He hit the rim of the shower, his arms and wings waving violently trying desperately to stay on the soap, but after whizzing around the shower tray once, he fell off, sliding across the shower floor and only stopping when the end of his tail got caught in the drain. Arrek tried to stand but his little head was spinning around and his tail was still stuck.

Alex came to the rescue and released his tail and quickly washed his face before he could get away. The little dragon stood there, now clean, and gave the soap a stare as he shot a flame at it. The soap just slid away.

Mummy came in with the finished robe for Arrek. It was beautiful in bright red with black trim and a black belt.

"That was quick, Mummy!" said Alex.

"Well, I had it made, I just needed to sort the arms, wings and length," she replied.

Alex put it on the little dragon.

"Oops!" said Mummy as the hood fell over his eyes. "I need to put a tack stitch in that."

Arrek felt good in his new robe and skipped off to the bedroom, keeping very close to the wall as he passed the stairs.

"I have had a text from Daddy to say he will be home this evening," said Mummy.

"Oh, wow!" said Alex. "That's great news. What time do we have to pick him up?"

"About eight o'clock," said Mummy.

"That's great, can Arrek come with us?"

"Well, we could take him," said Mummy, "but we will have to go to the pet shop first."

"Why, Mummy?" asked Alex.

"Well, I think we need to buy a small harness and lead so he doesn't get lost."

"What a great idea," said Alex. "I will settle him down for a sleep and then we can go to the shop."

When Alex went into the bedroom, Arrek was stalking a spider that was walking along the skirting board. Arrek heard her come in, glanced over his shoulder, winked, then looked back at the spider. His tongue shot out and Arrek had dinner!

When he had finished, Alex said, "Arrek, it's time for your rest."

Still in his new robe, he jumped in his bed. As Alex leaned in to settle him down, he gave her a big lick, then curled up and drifted off to sleep. Alex joined Mummy downstairs and they headed for the car together.

Alex hadn't been to the pet shop for a long time. In fact, the last time was when they went to buy George and that was several years ago. George was now a large tortoise, although, when he had first come home, he had been quite small. George lived out in the garden all summer and in a box full of straw in the boiler room during the winter. The pet shop was busy as people seemed to always bring their dogs with them. As Alex got out of the car, she was greeted by a large black Labrador called Shadow. Alex thought how friendly he seemed.

"Come on, Alex!" called Mummy. "We haven't got all day!"

Alex chased after Mummy who was now disappearing inside the shop. When Alex caught her up, she had her tape measure out and was measuring a small harness.

"Find a nice lead, Alex," Mummy said, "while I sort the harness."

"Okay, Mummy," said Alex and, a few minutes later, she reappeared with a nice orange one to match Arrek's chest.

"Good thinking, Alex," said Mummy who was now holding a very small orange harness. "What have you got there?" asked Mummy.

"It's a present for Arrek; he likes round things so I got him a small ball."

"It doesn't squeak, does it?" asked Mummy.

"No, I made sure it didn't."

"Okay," said Mummy. "Let's go and pay and get on home. I need to do dinner before we go to the airport."

"Okay, Mummy, let's get out of here."

So off they went to pay and then they headed home.

Mummy opened the front door and they went in.

"Have I got time for a quick chat with Noroth?" Alex asked.

"Dinner will be about fifteen minutes," said Mummy, "so don't be long."

"Okay, Mummy," said Alex as she disappeared upstairs.

Alex crept into the bedroom, as she could hear Arrek snoring, and she got out Noroth's box. Alex went into Mummy's room so as not to disturb Arrek. She got out the shell.

"Hi, Noroth, are you there?"

The shell started to glow and writing started to appear. 'Yes, I'm here, Alex. Is everything all right?'

"Yes, everything is fine. I just wanted to ask you a question."

'Okay,' said Noroth. 'What is it?'

"Well, Arrek has stopped shooting flames from his nose. It's coming from his mouth now. Is that normal?"

'Yes, it's quite normal. He is getting older and growing up. He will only use his mouth now to send flames.'

"Okay," said Alex.

The writing changed again. 'Just one other thing.'

"Yes?" said Alex.

'You don't have to worry about the flames. Dragons are very clever; the flames will only burn where he thinks they should go. If Arrek wanted to burn a hole in a piece of paper, that's all he would do, the rest of the paper would be fine. Do you understand, Alex?' said Noroth.

"Yes, I think so," said Alex.

'Have fun at the airport,' appeared in the shell and then it faded away.

Just then Mummy called, "Dinner's ready!"

Alex put the shell away and went downstairs.

"Everything all right?" asked Mummy.

"Yes, all okay, Mummy," said Alex.

After dinner, Alex got Arrek and carefully brought him downstairs. He was still in the robe and didn't want to take it off.

"Come on," said Alex, "You need to put this pretty harness on."

She showed it to Arrek. He shook his robe off and let Alex put the harness on him.

"We are going to the airport to meet Daddy," said Alex, "and you are coming too!"

Arrek jumped up and down in excitement.

"But you must wear this so that you will be attached to me and you won't get lost. Understand?" said Alex.

Arrek looked at her and winked. As they went to the door Alex saw Thomas on the fence in the front garden. Thomas was a nasty cat who was a bully and terrorised all the cats and some of the dogs in the street. Alex wondered what he would make of Arrek.

She put Arrek on the lead and went outside into the front garden. Thomas looked at Arrek and hissed. Arrek ignored Thomas which made him mad. He jumped off the fence and swiped Arrek across the nose. Arrek jumped and blue blood started to run from the scratch. Thomas crouched ready to strike again, but Arrek took one step backwards and focused hard on Thomas. Then a flame shot from Arrek's mouth straight between Thomas's ears and hitting the tip of his tail. The smell of singed fur filled the air. Thomas had a thin bald strip between his ears and the tip of his tail was also bald. There was a very loud "Meeeeeowwwww!" from Thomas as he disappeared back over the fence.

"What was all that about?" asked Mummy.

"Oh, just Mrs McKenzie's cat from number 23 meeting Arrek."

"You'd better clean that scratch up on Arrek's nose," said Mummy, seeing the trickle of blue blood as she shut the front door. "You can use the first aid kit in the car."

"Okay, Mummy will do."

Mummy opened the back door of the car and Alex jumped in, followed very closely by Arrek.

"Oh, Mummy, you have put my other booster seat in for Arrek!"

"Yes," said Mummy. "I thought it might stop him bouncing about if he could see out. Also, you can clip his harness to the seat belt so he is safe."

"Great, Mummy," said Alex as she made Arrek secure.

And with that, they headed off to the airport.

Chapter 9 Arrek at the Airport

They soon arrived at the airport; Arrek was getting very excited and trying to get out of the car. Mummy parked the car and came around to let both Alex and Arrek out.

"Hold on to him tight, Alex," said Mummy.

"I will," said Alex as they headed off across the car park towards the big glass doors. Just as they were about to enter the airport, Arrek saw it… well, not just it! When the automatic door opened, there were cobwebs and lots of them. Arrek pulled back on his lead, his tongue shot out and a spider disappeared into his mouth, then another, then a third.

"Mind your tongue in the door, Arrek," said Alex, as the little dragon let out a loud burp and two plumes of smoke came from his nostrils.

'Seems like a great place to come to eat,' thought Arrek.

"If he keeps on like that," said Mummy, "he will want us to get him a take-away."

Alex and Mummy laughed.

As they walked across the concourse towards the escalator, people looked and stared at the little dragon walking along. Arrek pulled himself up to look as tall and proud as he could.

'Anybody would think they had never seen a dragon before!' thought Arrek.

"Are you going to carry him down the escalator?" asked Mummy. But before Alex could answer, Arrek jumped on, quickly followed by Alex.

"Well, getting on was easy," said Mummy as they approached the bottom.

Arrek looked in horror as the steps went flat and silver teeth were eating them. He turned and started running away, but he wasn't getting anywhere. As he looked over his shoulder and saw the silver teeth catching up with him, Alex swept him up into her arms. Arrek looked her in the eye and gave her a big lick.

"Daddy's in Baggage Reclaim," said Mummy. "He has just texted. Let's go and get a drink."

And off they went to the coffee bar.

As Mummy went to order, the man behind the counter said, "No dogs in here!"

"He's not a dog," replied Alex, "he's a dragon."

"Oh, yeah?" said the man. "And I'm a monkey's uncle!" With that two flames shot past the man's ear, just close enough for him to feel the heat.

"Stop that, Arrek!" said Alex. "I'm sure the man will let us stay now."

"Sit in the corner out of the way," said the man.

Alex and Arrek headed off as Mummy got a coffee and some lemonade.

When they had finished their drinks, they headed to the arrivals area to wait for Daddy. They didn't have to wait long until Arrek spotted him and started jumping up and down.

"There he is, Mummy!" said Alex and off they all went to greet him.

"Hello," said Daddy, giving Mummy and Alex a kiss. "And what have we here?"

"Arrek has come to meet you."

And with that, the little dragon leaped into Daddy's arms and gave him a big lick.

"Come on," said Daddy, "let's get home."

So they left the baggage trolley and headed for the escalator.

"Arrek is really funny on the escalator, Daddy," said Alex. "He thought it was going to eat him. He was okay getting on, but didn't like getting off."

Daddy laughed. As they got to the escalator, Arrek didn't jump on it; he just stopped and looked up.

"Do you want to be carried?" asked Alex.

Arrek just winked and leaped up, not into her arms but onto the moving handrail. Arms and wings stretched out for balance.

"Mummy! Daddy! Arrek is surfing up the escalator."

Everyone laughed as they got to the top and Arrek jumped off doing a little somersault, getting tangled in his lead and ending up rolling on the floor.

"He is getting a cheeky little chap!" said Daddy as Alex untangled him.

"He certainly is," said Mummy as they walked out of the airport.

In the car on the way home, Daddy told them all about his trip and a strange card that he had found in his room.

"What was on the card?" said Mummy.

"Well, nothing when I picked it up. It was blank, but then like the shell, writing appeared on it with the name and address of a shop and the words, 'Your present for Alex'."

"Oh, wow!" said Alex. "Did you go?"

"Yes, I did go," said Daddy, "but not for a couple of days as I was busy with work. When I got there, I couldn't find the shop and no one knew of it."

"So I didn't get the present?" asked Alex.

"Be patient," said Daddy, "I haven't finished yet. I went back to the hotel. When I entered my room, there was another card on the floor, just as before with nothing on it.

"As I picked it up the writing appeared. It just said, 'Go back to the shop now. It will be there but hurry'. I headed straight out again. It was nearly midnight when I got there. As I walked in to the pitch-black alley, a faint light appeared. I walked towards it and, as I got near, the door opened and a lady said, "Come in, Roger. [Roger is Daddy's name] I have your present for Alex, but it's not to be opened until you get home." She gave me the package, said good bye and shut the door."

With that, Mummy pulled up outside the house.

"Have you got it, Daddy?" asked Alex.

"Yes," said Daddy, "and just how it was given to me."

They all went indoors and Mummy went to the kitchen to put the kettle on for a cup of tea for Daddy, as well as pouring an orange juice for Alex and a clean bowl of water for Arrek.

'Well, he has just eaten four spiders, so he must be thirsty,' thought Mummy.

Daddy, Alex and Arrek were in the lounge, unpacking Daddy's case and sorting out all the washing. As they got to the bottom, there was the parcel Daddy had brought home, wrapped in plain brown paper. Alex lifted it out. It was quite big and flat. She sat on the sofa with it.

"I wonder what's in here?" said Alex.

"You had better open it, darling," said Mummy as she came in the room.

But just then, writing started to appear.

"Is that you, Noroth?" asked Alex.

The writing said, 'No, I'm Walnort. I just deliver special packages to Dragon Keepers. Noroth told me that you are now ready for this. You must treasure it always.'

"What is it?" asked Alex.

'You will see when you open it. Just remember one thing – it must never get wet as it will never get dry,' and with that, Walnort and the writing disappeared.

Alex started to unwrap the parcel, but what was inside was one very big surprise!

Chapter 10: Arrek meets his ancestors

As Alex unwrapped the parcel, one large piece of material, two medium pieces and a smaller piece appeared.

Mummy looked and said, "That looks to me like a duvet cover with two pillowcases, but I don't know what the other is."

"I do," said Alex. "It's a dragon's duvet cover, but it's a very strange colour."

"It looks the same colour as the lamp shell did when you unpacked that, Alex," said Mummy.

"It looks huge to me," said Daddy.

"Yes, it does," said Mummy as Daddy disappeared upstairs to get Alex's duvet.

When Daddy came back, he had the pillows, duvet and Arrek's bed.

Mummy said, "It's going to be far too big for Alex's duvet."

But then something very strange started to happen. As Mummy got the duvet in the cover, it became the right size. The same thing happened with the pillowcases and with Arrek's bed. Then something even stranger started to happen. Arrek put his head right back and made a very strange sound. Three short bursts of flames came from his mouth, and the duvet, pillowcases and his bed started to change. Lots of pictures started to appear with names under them. The pictures were all of dragons.

"That's Ninarth the Dragon Lord and Kelarth the Great from Poland," said Alex.

"But who are all these others?" asked Daddy.

Holarth the Strong, Gathalk the Giver of Love, Florenth the Giver of Strength and many others appeared. Then Arrek moved closer and stared at a very beautiful dragon as her name appeared. Rieenpeya the Giver of life, mother of Arrek the Noble. Tears formed in the little dragon's eyes as he snuggled up close.

"Arrek the Noble!" gasped Alex. "Arrek, that's you, and that's your mummy!"

Arrek's picture appeared on the material. The duvet went dark as the last picture appeared. It was Erfolg, Arrek's wicked grandfather. The image of Erfolg was causing the picture of Nochiss to slowly disappear; Nochiss was grandmother to Arrek the Noble.

Arrek stood back as the image of Erfolg reared up looking vicious and threatening. Arrek took a deep breath, filling his lungs, and let out a noise. The flame from his mouth roared as it hit the image of Erfolg. The young dragon took Erfolg by surprise, and the powerful flame banished Erfolg for the rest of his life and he would never be seen again. There was a sort of strange cheer from the duvet, and Arrek looked really proud as he saw both Rieenpeya and Nochiss shed a tear.

"I think that there has been enough excitement in this house for one night. It's time you were all in bed. Let's get this bedding upstairs," said Mummy.

And with that, Alex and Daddy took Arrek, his bed, the pillows and duvet upstairs.

"When you're undressed, Alex," Mummy said, "you'd better pop down with Daddy and the shell; I think we should have a chat with Noroth before you go to bed."

"Okay, Mummy," Alex said.

"Good idea," said Daddy.

Alex took Arrek to clean his teeth and Daddy went to the bathroom to watch.

"He's very good at it," said Alex, as the proud little dragon was scrubbing all the soot off his fangs with the toothbrush. 'Too many flames tonight,' thought Alex, but didn't say anything as she didn't want to tell him off.

A few minutes later, the little dragon was in bed, snuggled up to the picture of Rieenpeya, his mother. Daddy, Alex and the shell joined an exhausted Mummy in the lounge.

"Well," said Mummy, "I think we had better ask Noroth if that is likely to happen again – it was all a bit scary!"

"You're right, Mummy," said Alex, getting the shell from its box.

"Hi, Noroth, are you there?" asked Alex.

The shell started to glow. 'Yes,' wrote the shell. 'I'm here and I see Walnort has been in touch.'

"Yes," said Alex.

'I'm glad your daddy got the parcel. I hope you like it.'

"It's beautiful," said Alex, "but we do have a few questions."

The writing changed. 'I thought you might have,' wrote the shell. 'Ask away and I will try to give you the answers that you're looking for.'

"Well, there seems to have been a bit of a fight between Erfolg and Arrek."

'Yes,' wrote Noroth, 'it was always going to happen, but we didn't expect it to happen just yet with Arrek being so young. But it is a great thing that you have witnessed tonight. What you have seen is young Arrek proving himself probably fifty years earlier than we ever expected.'

"What does this mean? Will it happen again?" asked Mummy.

The writing in the shell changed. 'No, it will never happen again. Arrek has tonight shown the Dragon World that he is and will remain the greatest dragon in living memory. He has banished Erfolg forever, protecting not only the whole of the Dragon World, but you, his family, too. I'm so glad we picked Alex to be his dragon keeper. The Dragon World is very content tonight and we will all sleep sounder in our beds. Goodnight,' wrote the shell, and faded away.

"Come on young lady," Mummy said to Alex. "Time you were in bed too; you must be exhausted."

"I'm very tired," said Alex.

"So am I," said Daddy. "It's been a long day."

"When you get upstairs, please put your washing on the landing," said Mummy. "I have all Daddy's and ours to do in the morning and the weather man says it will be nice tomorrow, so I can get it out on the line."

"Okay," said Alex. "No story tonight, Daddy. I'm too tired."

"I agree," said Daddy.

"And make sure you shut your bedroom door; we don't want Arrek wandering about."

"Okay, Mummy," said Alex and kissed them goodnight. When Alex got in her room, the little dragon was curled up, cuddling the picture of his mummy, fast asleep.

'Did the picture of Arrek's mummy just wink?' thought Alex. 'No, surely not.' With that, she jumped into bed, put out the light and drifted off to sleep.

Chapter 11: Arrek disappears in the kitchen

Mummy was up early the next morning, as she had a lot to do with all the washing from the week, and when Alex awoke the first load was already on the line.

"Hi, Mummy!" called Alex.

"Hello, darling." replied Mummy. "Did you and Arrek sleep all right?"

"Yes, thank you," said Alex. "Arrek is having a drink of water. Where is Daddy?"

"He has gone for a round of golf with Uncle Dennis and will be back around twelve o'clock," said Mummy. "Would you like some toast?"

"Yes, please, but I'm going in the shower first and so is Arrek. All that breathing fire seems to have left him sooty. He is coughing a bit today and little sooty smuts keep appearing."

"Good idea," said Mummy. "I will bring the toast up. What would you like on it?"

"Marmite, please; two slices," said Alex.

"Okay, and I have some stewing steak for Arrek."

"Great! Thanks, Mummy," said Alex.

Alex got the still snoring dragon out of his bed. He snuggled in and gave a wink and a little lick.

"Time you had a shower and cleaned your teeth again, you little sooty dragon!"

And with that, she picked up their robes and headed off to the bathroom. Alex cleaned her teeth with Arrek sitting on the edge of the hand basin cleaning his.

When Alex spat out, Arrek spat out. When Alex gargled, Arrek gargled, then Alex started giggling and so did Arrek.

"I've never heard you giggle before, Arrek," said Alex.

Arrek winked and jumped in the shower.

About fifteen minutes later, Mummy looked into the bathroom. Alex was in her bathrobe and was helping Arrek into his.

"Come on, you two, your breakfast is waiting."

"I'm ready now, Mummy," said Alex and off they all went to the bedroom, Arrek keeping very close to the wall as he walked past the stairs.

"Still not keen on the stairs, is he?" said Mummy.

"No," said Alex. Mummy collected up the towels and took them downstairs to put them in with the washing.

Alex ate her toast and got dressed while Arrek had his breakfast and an unsuspecting fly that happened to settle on his dinner bowl.

"Right!" said Alex. "We are going downstairs now."

And with that, Arrek jumped in her arms and hid his eyes.

At the bottom of the stairs Alex put Arrek down and went into the lounge. Arrek went towards the window that you can't see out of, with the mouth below it, and, as he approached, a large white thing came through it. Arrek attacked it and pieces went everywhere. It was the newspaper. There were sheets of it all over the place.

'Mmm,' he thought, 'perhaps that was a little bit over the top.'

Alex was laughing as she picked it up and put it back together.

"Come on, Arrek," said Alex. "Let's go and see how Mummy is getting on with the washing." So off they went to the kitchen.

"Hi, Mummy, can I help?" asked Alex.

"Yes, dear," replied Mummy, "you can help me peg this washing on the line. The next lot will be finished in a few minutes, then there are just towels and tea towels to do."

"Okay, Mummy," said Alex. "Now, you stay here, Arrek, I won't be long."

Mummy and Alex went into the garden with the washing.

Arrek was playing in the pile of towels when he heard them coming back, so he thought that he would have some fun and hide. Just as Mummy and Alex came in, the alarm on the washing machine went off and he dived under the towels to hide.

"I'll get the washing out," said Alex and, as she emptied the machine, Mummy scooped up the towels all in one go and pushed them into the machine, threw in the soap tablet and turned it on.

"Come on, Mummy, let's get this out, then I can play with Arrek."

"Okay," said Mummy and off they went back into the garden to hang the washing out.

As the water rushed in to the machine, Arrek was having great fun; it wasn't full of water, so he could always get his head out for air as it swished him backwards and forwards. But then it started to heat the water, slowly at first.

Mummy and Alex came back in. Alex called Arrek, but he was nowhere to be seen. They hunted everywhere but still nothing. Daddy walked in the front door. By now, Alex was getting frantic.

"What's the matter?" asked Daddy.

"It's Arrek," Mummy said, "We can't find him!"

"I'm sure that he is fine," said Daddy. "He's probably under the furniture."

"No," said Alex, "when he does that you can always see his tail and he blows smoke rings. He's not here!"

While Daddy, Mummy and Alex were searching, Arrek was getting a little warm. He decided the only thing to do was to make the water disappear and, being a clever little dragon, he knew, if he turned it into steam, it would all go away. So he aimed flames at the water, so as not to damage the washing. After a few moments, Daddy noticed that he couldn't see into the kitchen. He rushed in, looking at the machine, which was now letting off large clouds of steam. As he looked in, he saw Arrek looking out. Arrek saw Daddy and gave him a cheeky wink.

"Alex! Mummy! I've found him."
They both rushed into the kitchen,
"Where is he, Daddy?"
Daddy pointed to the dragon, who was now on slow spin.

"Daddy! Daddy! Please get him out!" cried Alex, as the dragon went to medium spin.

"Don't worry," said Daddy. "I have cancelled the programme; it will stop in a minute."

As soon as it did and the door could be opened, the little dragon fell out. He tried to stand but wobbled a lot before landing on his bottom, eyes spinning and soapsuds on his nose and head. He tried to blow flames through his nostrils, but all that came out were soap bubbles. Alex picked him up and Mummy grabbed a towel from the washing machine, but something had happened to the towel.

All the steam that Arrek had made got all the towels very hot and they had now shrunk. They were no longer big bath towels, but Arrek-size bath towels! Mummy, Daddy and Alex laughed, as Arrek winked and managed to blow a plume of soap bubbles into the air.